Harriet Eleanor King

Ballads of the North, and Other Poems

Harriet Eleanor King

Ballads of the North, and Other Poems

ISBN/EAN: 9783744787628

Printed in Europe, USA, Canada, Australia, Japan

Cover: Foto ©Andreas Hilbeck / pixelio.de

More available books at **www.hansebooks.com**

BALLADS OF THE NORTH

ETC.

BALLADS OF THE NORTH

AND OTHER POEMS

BY

HARRIET ELEANOR HAMILTON KING

AUTHOR OF 'THE DISCIPLES' 'ASPROMONTE'
'A BOOK OF DREAMS' ETC.

LONDON

KEGAN PAUL, TRENCH, & CO., 1 PATERNOSTER SQUARE

1889

CONTENTS.

BALLADS OF THE NORTH.

LONDON STREETS.

MISCELLANEOUS.

BALLADS OF THE NORTH

THE BALLAD OF THE MIDNIGHT SUN.

1883.

PART I.

THE still white coast at Midsummer,
  Beside the still white sea,
Lay low and smooth and shining
  In this year eighty-three ;
The sun was in the very North,
  Strange to see.

The walrus ivory lay in heaps
  Half-buried in the shore,
The slow stream slid o'er unknown beds
  Of golden ore,
Washings of amber to the beach
  Light waves bore.

Sprays of white, like foam-flowers,
    Betwixt the skies and seas,
Swayed and poised the sea-gulls
    In twos and threes,
Clustered like the stars men call
    Pleiades.

The white marsh-flowers, the white marsh-grass
    Shimmered amid the grey
Of the marsh-water—mirrored
    Over and under, they
Stood stiff and tall and slender,
    All one way.

The upper spake to the lower,
    'Are ye, or do ye seem?'
Out of the dim marsh-water
    Glided as in a dream
The still swans down a distance
    Of moonbeam.

The willow-warbler dropped from the spray
    Sweet notes like a soft spring shower,
There was a twitter of building birds
    In the blackthorn bower,
All broken from bare to gossamer
    In an hour.

A garden white lay all the land
    In wreaths of summer snow,
The heart of the year upspringing
    Swift and aglow,
In pale flame and slender stalk,
    Smooth and low.

The white heath and white harebell
    Let their chimes rise and fall,
The delicate sheets of wood-sorrel
    Unfolded all,
For a bed of bridal—
    Or a pall?

Powdered with pearl, auriculas,
   And beds of snowdrop sheen,
Frostwork of saxifrage, and fair balls
   Of winter green :
There was no room for foot to pass
   In between.

One only pink, the fragrant bloom
   Of all blooms boreal,[1]
Every face of every flower
   With looks funereal
Bent to earth, and faintly
   Flowering all.

Down in the closely crowded camp
   Of the fresh snowdrops lay,
Fever and famine-stricken,
   None his name to say,
Sick to death, a traveller
   Cast away.

---

[1] *Linnea borealis.*

Brother might be of Balder
 The beautiful, the bold,
By Northern stature and by limbs'
 Heroic mould,
And the uncurled faint hair
 Of pale gold.

Faintly the words were uttered,
 Low, betwixt moan and moan :
' Here in the wilderness,
 Lost and alone,
I die, and far away,
 Hast thou known ?

' Fame, and story of wonder,
 Wind of rumour had blown
My name to thine, my feet
 Up to thy throne :
What has the world been since ?---
 Thee alone.

'I passed and bowed before thy face,
  And once thine eyes met mine ;
Once I have kissed thy hand ;—
  Hast thou no sign ?
Here with my last sad breath
  I am thine.'

The white hares nibbled fearlessly
  Among the tender green ;
The silver foxes stayed and watched,
  Quick-eyed and keen ;
The little ermine soft of foot
  Stole between.

But the white world changed and quickened
  To a red world, the same ;
For with splendour as of sunset
  And sunrise flame,
From the highest heaven to the lowest,
  Midnight came.

The pulsing colours of the sky
   Deepened and purified ;
All glorious chords of gold and red
   Struck out and died ;
Stilled in one heavenly harmony
   Spread out wide,

In one ethereal crimson glow ;
   As if the Rose of Heaven
Had blossomed for one perfect hour,
   Midsummer Even,
As ever in the mystic sphere
   Of stars seven.

An opening blush of purest pink,
   That swiftly streams and grows
As shoreward all the liquid waste
   Enkindled flows,
Every ripple of all the sea
   Rose on Rose.

—Through the heavens of midnight
   Came a bitter cry,
Flesh and spirit breaking,
   Mortal agony ;
Died away unanswered
   Through the sky.—

But all the dim blue South was filled
   With the auroral flame,
Far out into the southward land
   Without a name
That dreamed away into the dark,—
   When One came,

Suddenly came stepping,
   Where the roseate rift
Of the boreal blossoms
   Crossed the snowy drift
In a trailing pathway,
   Straight and swift.

Her robes were full and silken,
　Her feet were silken-shod,
In sweeping stately silence,
　Serene she trod
The starry carpets strewing
　The soft sod.

The eyes of the veronica
　Looked out and far away,
A golden wreath around her head
　Of light curls lay,
And rippled back a shining shower,
　In bright array.

About her neck the diamonds flashed
　In rivers of blue fire ;
But whiter her soft shoulders than
　Her white attire,
And tenderer her tender arms
　Than heart's desire.

She fronted full the crimson flood
  Of all the Northern space,
And all the hue of all the sky
  Was in her face ;
The Rose of all the World has come
  To this place.

A vision of white that glowed to red
  With the fire at heaven, at heart,—
Nor paused nor turned,—but straight to him
  Who lay apart,
On she came, and knelt by him,—
  Here thou art !

At the first hour after midnight,
  As in the eider's nest,
The weary head sank soft into
  A heavenly rest ;
Is it a bed of roses,—
  Or her breast ?

At the second hour the cold limbs
    Felt comfort unaware ;
Flickering, a golden glow
    Warmed all the air :
Is it the hearth-flame lighted,—
    Or her hair ?

At the third hour, round the faint heart
    Failing in chill alarms,
Is it some silken coverlet
    Still wraps and warms
In close and closer clasping ?—
    Or her arms ?

At the fourth hour, to the wan lips
    There came a draught divine :
Some last reviving cup poured out
    Of hallowed wine,—
Or is it breath of hers
    Mixed with thine ?

At the fifth hour all was dimness
    Alike to him and her ;
One low and passionate murmur
    Still moved the air ;
Is it the voice of angels,—
    Or her prayer ?

At the sixth hour there stirred only
    The soft wave on the beach ;
Two were lying stilly,
    Past sound or speech,
Fair and carven faces,
    Each by each.

PART II.

The Summer Palace stood by night
    Lit up in dazzling sheen,
The doors unfolded, and the pomp
    Stirred in between ;
—To a burst of royal music
    Came the Queen.

Her eyes like stars of speedwell
  Shone down the great saloon ;
She came, and all before her
  Knew it was June ;
The passing of her presence
  Was too soon.

The little curls around her head
  Were all her crown of gold,
Her delicate arms drooped downward
  In slender mould,
As white-veined leaves of lilies
  Curve and fold.

All in white,—not ivory
  For young bloom past away,—
Blossom-white, rose-white,
  White of the May ;
'Twixt white dress and white neck,
  Who could say ?

She moved to measure of music,
　　As a swan sails the stream ;
Where her looks fell was summer,
　　When she smiled was a dream ;
All faces bowing towards her
　　Sunflowers seem.

O the rose upon her silent mouth,
　　The perfect rose that lies !
O the roses red, the roses deep,
　　Within her cheeks that rise !
O the rose of rapture of her face
　　To our eyes !

The tall fair Princes smile and sigh
　　For grace of one sweet glance,
The glittering dancers fill the floor,
　　The Queen leads the dance ;
The dial-hands to midnight
　　Still advance.

Dance down to the melting music !
  Hark to the viols' strain !
Their notes are piercing, piercing,
  Again, again ;
The pulse of the air is beating
  Throbs of pain.

Does the dancing languish slower ?
  Oh, the soft flutes wail and sigh ;
In silver falling and calling,
  They seek reply ;
And the heart is sinking, sinking,
  Why, ah why ?

Oh, the high harp-strings resounding !
  So long, so clear they are :
A cry is ringing in heaven
  From star to star,
Rising sharper and fainter
  From afar.

C

The Queen has danced from end to end ;
  Oh, the candles burn so bright !
But her blue eyes look far away
  Into the night ;
And the roses on her cheeks and lips
  Have grown white.

Oh, why is the Queen so pale to-night ?
  And why does silence fall,
As one by one they turn to her,
  Upon them all ?
Whence comes that cold wind shivering
  Down the hall ?

The hour draws close to midnight,
  The banquet board is spread ;
The lamps are lit, the guests are set,
  The Queen at the head :
For the feasting at kings' tables
  Grace be said !

The shaded light of rubies
   Streams from every part
Down the golden supper ;—
   Who is sick at heart ?
Oh, hush ! for the Queen is listening,
   Lips apart.

She sits with wide and open eyes,
   The wine-cup in her hand ;
And all the guests are ill at ease,
   Nor understand ;
Is it not some enchanted
   Strange far land ?

The twelve long strokes of midnight
   With clash and clang affright ;
The rose-glow seems to darken
   Before their sight ;
But the Queen has swooned back heavily,
   Cold and white.

They lifted her, a burden
　　Like broken lily-flowers ;
They laid her on her own bed,
　　Within her bowers ;
They mourned, and they tended her,
　　For six hours.

At the first hour after midnight,
　　The Queen nor spoke nor stirred ;
At the second, by her bedside,
　　No breath they heard ;
They said, ' Is she living ? '
　　At the third.

At the fourth hour they watched sadly
　　At her feet and her head ;
At the fifth, standing idle,
　　No word they said ;
At the sixth, ' Bring candles
　　For one dead.'

Swept low down across the East,
   Through the morning grey,
A flock of white clouds swiftly,
   Dim, far away ;
Like a flight of white wings :—
   What were they ?

Through the palace suddenly,
   Through every floor,
Wailed a wind and whistled,
   Shook every door,
Rattled through the windows,
   Then passed o'er.

And as they stood with tapers tall
   Around the Queen, there came
A soft and far-off fluttering
   Over her frame,
And from between her sleeping lips,
   One faint flame.

They take her hand, they call on her,
　　She answers them likewise ;
She sits upright, she looks around,
　　With her blue eyes,
And a smile as of thy secrets,
　　Paradise !

　　　　　　　.　　　.　　　.

Winter is here, and has not brought
　　The Traveller of renown ;
Why has he not come back again
　　To court and town ?
Rumours and questionings pas
　　Up and down.

Is it only the wolves of the Northland
　　Know where his bones lie white ?
Only the swans could tell us,
　　In southward flight ?
Is it only the wind could whisper
　　To the night ?

The Queen sits still and smiling,
　　She hears the talk prevail,
She speaks no word, she gives no glance,
　　She tells no tale ;
In the golden shadow always
　　She is pale.

THE HAUNTED CZAR.

ROMAN ROMANOVITCH, forgive
   The vilest of all men and worst !
Amid this death-in-life I live ;
   Hear me but once whom thou hast curst !
My doom, my anguish I confess ;—
Mercy on me the merciless !

Roman Romanovitch, there peals
   Imperial music of the march
Along my pathway, as it wheels
   On from triumphal arch to arch :
They say my face is wan and white ;—
Thy cries ring round me day and night.

Roman Romanovitch, my bed
   Is deep with down, and flaxen-white ;
The fresh and ghastly stains of red
   Are wet against my cheeks all night ;
Where'er I turn, where'er I toss,
Some stiffening limb creeps cold across.

In purple and in gold I stand,
   Amid the worship of the crowd ;
Their hearts, their lives are in my hand ;
   The people say that I am proud :
I in the dust beneath thy feet,
Roman Romanovitch, entreat !

A dying voice of torture wails
   Through all the church's chants divine ;
It rises—and the banquet pales ;
   I drench the darkness down with wine ;
But when my lips are at the brink,
'Tis blood I taste, and blood I drink.

In the same hour, upon me broke
  In sweat of agony and fear
The act I never could revoke,
  For ever haunting eye and ear.
Yes, years are past—and long ago
I see a sunrise on the snow ;

And thou and I in that low light,
  And a few more, of armed men ;
—Helpless and bound—but I upright ;
  None but my slaves about us then ;
My word their law, my will their guide :
—But there was no man on thy side.

Thou, martyr just and innocent,
  Against me sworn, and it was well ;
Thou the avenging angel sent,
  I the black instrument of hell.
But here I have thee :—spare thy breath !—
Long shalt thou call in vain on death.

Shriek after shriek rings through the North ;
  My laughter answers every cry ;
Prayer after prayer sobbed feebly forth ;
  Pray on, pray on, for it is I !
At last—O God !—the curses fall ;
My God, I hear—Thou hearest all.

Did it not end ? Do I not know ?
  Was it not I who did this thing ?
Was there not silence in the snow
  Between us, and a mightier King ?
I think at last those lips were dumb ;—
Why will their cries not cease to come ?

I see thee,—no, it is not thou !
  I saw thee once, and thou wast fair ;
A step like mine, an angel's brow ;—
  But what is this, that ghastly there
Droops to my feet, all dark and wet ?
Lift up thy face ! Let me forget !

It is not thou, I know full well,
   This spectre my own sins have made ;
This will go with me down to Hell,
   Whilst thou in Paradise art laid ;
Oh, come thyself, and cast behind
This, horrible and deaf and blind !

Oh, if thou couldst but look on me,
   Roman Romanovitch, thy heart
Would melt for very charity,
   Among the angels where thou art ;
Thou couldst not turn thine eyes and see,—
Ah God, did I not look on thee ?

Did not God make us, I and thou ?
   Have pity even for His sake !
My hair is bleached upon my brow,
   At every rose's fall I shake ;
My eyes, they say, are wild and wide ;—
O Ghost, at last be satisfied !

Roman Romanovitch, we two,
  Are we not men of flesh and blood?
Ah mangled flesh and blood, too true,
  They cry against me up to God.
Thou hast me in a grip so sure;—
Oh, how can heart of man endure!

Had we not mothers, both of us?
  Were we not born by ways the same?
Nay, I unworthy to be thus
  The son of woman, whence I came
Must be the way I know too well,
The way I go, the gate of hell.

Did not Christ die for thee and me?
  Ah, not for me! 'Twas I who slew!
I pierced, I nailed Him to the tree;
  He was with thee, He held thee through:
He left me then;—but thou, my Saint,
Against me pourest thy complaint

Within His arms, upon His breast ;
   His tears have washed and made thee white
Of all thy cruel wounds, and drest
   Thy swoonèd eyes again to light ;
For very pity all this while
He wept until He saw thee smile.

Oh, visit me, and let me pay
   With blood, and all thy justice take !
I supplicating writhe and pray
   For this absolving judgment's sake.
Not once, but for a thousand years,
Scourge me in blood and shame and tears.

Oh, strike, but only do not spare !
   Before thy hands I kneel, I fall ;
My flesh in stripes of crimson tear.
   Still, still to kiss thy feet I crawl ;
Past sense, past moans, but this to win,
Leave me not, pardon not my sin !

Wilt thou not hear?   Wilt thou not heed?
  In vain, in vain !—no hand but thine
Can heal or hurt ;—this ermine weed
  Still wraps me soft ; this crown of mine
Burns on my brows, and no one stirs
Round me but delicate flatterers.

Ah no, the fires of hell begin
  For me, unpurged, unshriven below ;
Thy deeper justice thou must win,
  The soul and not the body's woe ;
And what am I, that I should dare
The suffering of the saints to share ?

Thy bitter moans, that could not wring
  One moment's respite from my hate ;—
They called Him, and He came, thy King,
  But round me hell lies desolate :
If He were here,—too late, alas !
His feet no more this way will pass.

For could He come, His ears would pierce
   A bitterer, more heartrending moan ;
Where coiling serpents mingled fierce,
   Gnaw with fresh fangs through breast and bone;
Undying anguish wept and wailed,
Unheard, unanswered, unavailed.

Beneath the Altar yet they cry,
   Avenge us, Lord !—ah, do they know
They *are* avenged ? that in reply
   The swords through soul and spirit go ?
How many ages past and gone,
And still those souls keep crying on !

It is not for the torments run,
   Nor for the torments yet to be ;
But that I know what I have done,
   But that whom I have slain I see ;
It is for very love of thee
That my heart breaks in agony.

Alas, my brother, all the years
   Our souls together may not save ;
I may not water with my tears
   The grass that grows above thy grave ;
Thy very bones would stir and cry
With horror at me, drawing nigh.

O sweet, O sacred limbs, yes mine !
   For my heart holds them passionately ;
It is thy home, it is thy shrine,
   Though never may I reach to thee ;
To kiss thy feet I could not dare,
Thou even sleeping unaware.

Might I but watch, one hour of all,—
   Upon thy brows the least caress,
The lightest touch of love should fall
   Too roughly for my tenderness ;
Nor should disturb them, wandering by,
The blue wings of the butterfly.

To wait upon thee from afar,
　　To serve thee to thy lowest need,
Thy slave more fond than mothers are,
　　Although thy scorn were all my meed ;
— O dream too deep for my despair,
But once to touch thy golden hair !

I have no Christ -- I cannot kneel
　　To any, my beloved, but thee,
My mocked, my murdered one ; to feel
　　Thy pardon first !   It may not be.
No more.   Did I not hear thee pray
So long, so long, to me that day ?

Roman Romanovitch, I bow
　　Beneath thy curse ; no more I strive ;
I do not ask thy pity now,
　　Thou willest it, with soul alive.
What else is left me to atone ?
Have all thy will !. I am thine own.

Yet, even at the last, there streams
  Something like hope into my heart ;
I hold it fast within my dreams,
  That hour when I shall have my part ;
Down in the depth of all, I know,
Stronger than death, it must be so.

Once we must meet, however long
  The bead-roll of the centuries
Is counted by the Planet's Song ;
  The dead in Christ shall first arise ;
And I no more may hide my head,
That day when Hell gives up her dead.

The earth and heaven in thunders flee
  Before His face : each awful page
Unrolls of human history,
  Written in blood from age to age ;
Then Christ, the Slain and Risen anew,
Shall speak and judge between us two.

And first to me, outcast, who stand,
  Nor dare to look on Him or thee,
Nor meet thy holy eyes and grand,
  Amidst thy shining company,
The awful Judge will turn and say :
' Most miserable man, to-day

' The sum of all thy scarlet sin
  Is written up, and found no more ;
And thou snow-white may'st enter in
  My Temple—am not I the Door ?—
And by that way, that door, thy strife
Of penitence hath led to life.

' Do I not rule above the stars,
  To bind or loose from any curse ?
Against me Hell hath got no bars,
  No spaces hath the universe ;
Thy weeping still was in my ears
Through all the music of the spheres.

' But thou didst mourn and I did mourn,
  Together mourning thy disgrace,
In thy dark prison-house forlorn,
  Though never couldst thou see My face ;
Nor hast thou known a Victim bleeds,
A Priest for ever intercedes.

' Baptism of water and of fire
  Each soul of My redeemed must prove ;—
Oh, drowned amidst Love's anguish dire,
  And burnt amidst the flames of Love,
Come unto Me at last, and rest
Long-lost, long-loved, upon My breast !

' And thou, O Martyr merciless,
  Thou who so long from age to age
Hast shared serene in blessedness
  Among the Saints their heritage,
The crimson crown, the deathless palm,—
No looking back disturbed thy calm.

' The hands of angels carried thee
   To Paradise, and dried thy tears ;
The leaves of that immortal Tree
   Have healed thy wounds these many years
Beside the living water's stream
Lying in one unbroken dream.

' Short was thy pain, and long thy rest,
   Earth was thy loss, and heaven thy gain ;
Oh, safe and sheltered with the blest,
   No after-thought didst thou retain,
Wrapt in My love, and didst forget
The soul thou mightest succour yet.

' Thy peace was won, thy triumph crowned :
   Hath Love no thought for them that slew ?
Love in the Highest, in the Profound,
   Crucified every day anew.—
Where Love is, there must Suffering be ;
O Unforgiven, depart from Me.'

Then will I spring forth, then will seize
   My one last moment of all time ;
' Not me, but him, Lord, take with these !
   Mine was his crowning and his crime ;
A martyr made by pangs so sore,
As froze his heart for evermore.

' He is Thine own ; he has but slept ;
   Now he will wake and love again ;
So long to him in vain I wept,
   He, too, at last must weep, —a rain
That reconciles him to Thy heart.
Take back Thine own,—as I depart.'

Then surely, over the abyss,
   Roman Romanovitch, I see
Thee, glorious, bending with one kiss
   For me, accursèd, even me.
Thine eyes forgive me from the brink
At last, as out of sight I sink.

THE IRISH FAMINE.

BANTRY, 1847.

I WILL not speak of the famine, the terrible year that
 fell ;
We lived through it ; what one has lived through, one
 does not always tell :—
The hard months, the long months, the months that
 were sinking and sore,
Till the fever closed over us all, for the living could
 bear no more.

The Winter was over ; but Spring—that never would
 come again,
For a handful of food was not left, nor a spoonful for
 those in pain,

Who lay, the dying and sick, in the fever, bare on the
    floor,
While the starving children, like wolves, prowled
    round and cried at the door.

Half were dead—rest their souls !—but their bodies
    might not rest well,
For hands were not left to bury them,—heaped
    they fell
In the open pits together, hundreds, naked and
    cold ;
The rest were waiting to follow, our time was nearly
    told.

In the beginning of April, the day I sickened, came
    down
The rumour of some strange doctor arrived in the
    town ;
He came,—but what matter to us, who already were
    half in the grave ?
It was food, not medicine we wanted,—it was too late
    to save.

I cannot tell how he came,—as the morning breaks
 from the sea ;
'Twas a mortal man they told me,—it might or it
 might not be,—
He came,—but my eyes were dazzled,—a glint of
 gold there gleamed,
And though I lay in the fever, of the Saints in Heaven
 I dreamed.

I have heard of the Angel of Death—but this was
 the Angel of Life,
Young, and smiling, and slender, and stripped as it
 were to the strife,
To the wrestle by day and by night with the Terror
 that held us before,
For Death and Despair fled away as he came in at
 the door.

He had neither silver nor gold, he had neither name
 nor fame,
He had nothing at all in the world but the bag in his
 hand as he came,

And a barrel of meal for a gift that was sent to him
    by a friend,
But that was a good while after, when things had
    begun to mend.

But there was a hand by day, and there was a step by
    night,
In the huts where they lay on the earth without fire
    or candle-light,
And a voice that spoke through the dark, and a breast
    upon which to lean,
Close, close in the shivering sickness, and the sorrow-
    ful sighs between.

He held to their lips the cold water, they drank it and
    they revived ;
He bent down over the dying, they looked in his eyes
    and lived ;
And still, as the unseen arrows flew ever more fast and
    thick,
There was one that battled alone for the lives of all
    the sick.

He did battle alone, and he won ;—scarce one died
after he came ;

They fell, they sickened by hundreds ; he saved them
all the same.

'To God be the glory,'—he said so,—as for three
months, night and day,

He lived and he moved among us till the fever
passed away.

The Famine was over too, and like the dove to the
ark,

Hope came back to the earth, and of life to our breasts
a spark ;

We were weak, we were wan in the sun, but there we
all stood that day

Safe and well—ah the sorrowful moment ! when he
was to go away.

It was not a fine sight, truly, we were but poor folks
at best,

He was all there was to look at, nothing to say for the
rest ;

There was not much to speak of in clothes, and what
    little there was was torn ;
But his Reverence was there in black, very decent, if
    somewhat worn.

And he stepped up and spoke for us all, 'Sir, if I may
    make so bold,
In the name of these poor people whom you see here,
    young and old,
(And they wouldn't be here now, saving the excellent
    deeds you have done),
We wish to present our respects and our thanks to
    you, everyone.

' We have come through a time of trouble—but many
    did not come through,—
And we who are saved alive are all of us saved by
    you ;
To God and the Saints be the glory, and praises for
    evermore,
And those who are dead were sorry that you didn't
    arrive before.

'And we'll always be wishing you well, Sir, by the holy
    Peter and Paul,
(Though it's always Paul you speak by, and never
    poor Peter at all),
And myself will pray to St. Peter, that when you come
    to the gate,
He'll be pleased and proud to see you, and you
    needn't have long to wait.

'And nothing have we to give you, and you are poor
    as we,
But that will not last long, I'm thinking, for you have
    the luck as we see ;
But the blessing, the best of blessings,—the true
    heart's love and the prayer
Of those who were ready to perish—will follow you
    everywhere.

'And as you have dealt with us, Sir, in our time of
    trouble and woe,
May the Lord Himself deal with you wherever your
    road may go ;

And this is a sad day for us, that we must lose you
    indeed,
But never can we forget you ; and we bid you now
    good-speed.'

Then old Aileen took up speaking—ah ! she was the
    woman, the wise,
She could tell (though she never told them) the names
    of the stars in the skies,
And the midsummer midnight moonwort she could
    find and use for a charm,
Ninety years old and upwards, whom the fever could
    not harm.

'The seventh son of a seventh son ;—but this was a
    wondrous birth,
The seventeenth babe of his mother, and she no
    more on the earth ;
And now he is parting from us, nor his face may we
    more behold ;
So listen to me for the last time, to the words of me
    who am old.

' Our life is writ in the stars, and the stars their courses
     must run ;
But God will be shining in heaven when all their
     courses are done ;
And what is written is written, and fate our footsteps
     debars,
For we are the dust of the earth, as the earth is the
     dust of the stars.

'We have done some work together ; I have taken
     your hand in mine,
My old eyes have looked it over, and have read it line
     by line ;
And oh ! I see the great things, the wonderful things,
     the true,
That wait thee, O young man, yonder, and the work
     that thou hast to do.

' We are poor, we are naught in the world, we are
     little wanted here,
Perhaps it were best for all that we should but dis-
     appear ;

You did not think so, you came to us the lowest
  and least,
You saved us, you smiled upon us, you turned our
  famine to feast.

'But oh ! in the times to come, it will not be such as
  we !
Too great are the multitudes waiting, too long are the
  lines I see ;
They have looks that are not ours, they have thoughts
  we have not known,
Great and proud ones are among them, but with sorrows of their own.

'Oh, the hands that reach for comfort, oh, the feeble
  feet that press,
Oh, the hearts whose moans are breaking through the
  hour of their distress,
Oh, the eyes that turn in anguish seeking thine amidst
  their tears,
Hast thou all this burden on thee, and for all this
  length of years ?

' Hast thou all this glory on thee ?—that thy touch
    can loose and bind,
That despair awaits thy coming and deliverance stays
    behind,
That as thy daily passing leaves a daily track of light
Through the city, hearts, praying God for thee, must
    follow out of sight.

' Thank God for thee ! it echoes like a singing of souls
    in peace ;
Up and up a pathway shining brighter still as days
    increase,
Farther than I can follow, where the golden stairs
    ascend ;
We sang it first to God for you—angels sing it at the
    end.

' And thy strength shall be made perfect, the giver as
    the gift,
The head that is ever the highest, the step that is sure
    as swift ;

And the sun that knoweth no setting out of thine eyes
  shall shine,
And the Spirit of the Comforter shall ever dwell with
  thine.

' And you that have here no mother,—but, O my son,
  my son !
Methinks that the Blessed Mary looked on just such
  another one ;—
Methinks there were days in a lifetime when she forgot her fear,
As she saw the face that I see, and heard the voice
  that I hear !

' That face,—the dying faces are upturned to catch
  its light,
And fainting spirits hang round it to be quickened
  with new delight ;
But my heart outruns, as hers did, all the praising and
  the power,
And sees further, and cries in anguish—God help
  thee through that hour !

E 2

'Shall I pray to the Saints in Heaven for thee, who
    thyself art a Saint on earth?

Shall I pray to the Blessed Mother? nay, she smiled
    down at thy birth ;

To the Father of Spirits, the Highest, the cry of our
    hearts must be,

Give Thy best to this one belovèd, and let him not
    fall from Thee.

'Ah, how long is the road and how toilsome, or ever
    we come to rest !

But the last of straits was the sorest, and the last of
    sights was the best :

And now the hard times are over, and my work in
    the world is done ;

But I thank the Lord He has spared me to behold
    thy face, my son.'

The young man spoke not a word, as he stood before
    old Aileen ;

But he stooped bareheaded, and kissed her hand, like
    the hand of a queen ;

And there was not an eye that was dry of old or of
    young in the crowd,

As he passed out of sight and was gone, and the
    weeping was long and loud.

ALL SOULS' DAY.

WE drave across the Ocean to the West,
    On one November night of storm and rain ;
When morning dawned the winds were laid to rest,
    And quiet was the main.

And in the lull of the day-dawning dim
    A stranger stood on the deck and looked around,
And lordly spake to the Captain asking him,
    ' Whither is this ship bound ? '

And the Captain answered, ' Sir, we sail on yonder,
    Straight onward to the Islands of the Blest,
To the Haven of the Saints who went before us,
    Far in the farthest West.'

' And whom do you carry on your good ship forward?'
  'Valiant hearts, and full of faith are every one,
That will not fail till they reach the land of glory,
  Past the setting of the sun.'

' The way is long,' said the stranger musing inly,
  'Yea,' said the Captain, 'and a perilous way ;
With the storm, the deep, the dark, the air's dominion,
  We must battle night and day.'

'I am here,' said the other, 'to conduct, if any
  Will forsake the blessed quest, and tarry here ;
On this night alone I pass my post, and challenge
  Whomsoever may draw near.

' Here lies the country invisible and haunted
  Of All Souls, the innumerable, the sad,
And the night is here, and the morning when is granted
  That some message may be had.

' All night their shadowy shores were round you lying,
　　Albeit with holden eyes you marked them not,
Around you streamed the anguish and the sighing
　　Of those whom ye forgot.

' And if any here will stay and break their voyage,
　　I have come to be their convoy thitherward,
Though the place be desolate and full of weeping,
　　I will be their guide and guard.'

But the Captain spake, ' Not one of these assembled
　　Will turn back disheartened from the Glorious Way ;
There lies our path across the utmost ocean ; '
　　With one voice they answered, ' Yea ! '

And the other said, ' Are there none whom ye re-
　　member,
　　Who the feast of All the Saints may never share ?
Are there none who think on you, and ask forgiveness,
　　Yet to hope it do not dare ? '

Then I spake, because the face of power and pity
    Arrested and subdued me to his mind,
' Let these pass on unto the Golden City,
    But I will stay behind.'

He took my hand, and in a moment after
    We two upon the waves were all alone,
In a small boat that swiftly stemmed the waters,
    And the tall ship was gone.

And the grave ferryman asked, as I sat wondering,
    ' Grieve you not for the lost track of the Blessed
      Dead,
For the vision of All Saints, and all their splendour ? '
    ' Nay, mine were no Saints,' I said.

And I asked him, ' In your lost land and forsaken,
    Is there no hope, is it evermore the same ?
Hath there not any come to bring good tidings ? '
    ' Yea,' he said, ' once One came.'

'And from this country is there no departing?
   Is there no day of deliverance for All Souls?'
'Nay, I know not of the times,' he answered sighing,
   'Seals are upon those scrolls.'

Now the day was breaking, and the light grew clearer,
   Yet no glow of sunrise swept across the sky,
But a deep, sad blue coloured all the air and water,
   And the land, as we drew nigh.

In the blue of the hyacinth rose a hundred miles,
   Dark, and a darkling shadow across the bay ;
In the blue of the larkspur lay a thousand isles,
   Open and low to the dawning of the day.

And the distant sky was cloudy blue and tender,
   Not as the light of the sun makes blue the day ;
And his garments were dark-blue who sat before me,
   And light-blue was the spray

Of his oars, and all the morn melted in mystery
  Of some new life begun, of some unknown sense
And the face before me grew more beatific,
  And the low light more intense ;

And the world grew magical and hushed in wonder,
  And the gliding dream grew sweeter and more
    sweet ;
And I cried, 'Oh, what shore is this where we are
    landing?
  Whom are you taking me to meet?'

FATHER MACKONOCHIE.

ROSE-RED o'er Ballachulish
  The sunset dies away,
And glorious to the last expands
  The short December day ;
The purple islands of the West
  Stretch down the ocean way ;
The great and lonely mountain-land
  Looms inland ghostly-grey.

Suddenly with the evening
  The snow begins to fall,
And wailing voices of the North
  In the wild winds to call ;

And night wears on, and still they wait,
   Nor hear within the hall
Thy homeward steps, O father
   And friend, beloved of all !

Oh, dark upon Loch Leven
   Comes down the winter night ;
The desert spirits that love not man
   The lonely hills affright ;
The blinding whirlwinds and the snow
   Beat out all sound and sight,
No moon is there, nor stars to give
   The wanderer any light.

Oh, many on wild winter nights
   Have been out here too late,
And left among the haunted glens
   A hearthstone desolate ;
Poor men and women, none have marked
   Their name or their estate ;
And now the father of the flock
   Has come to share their fate.

Oh, awful is the wilderness,
　　And pitiless the snow ;
But down in dim St. Alban's
　　The seven lamps burn aglow,
And softly in the Sanctuary
　　The priest moves to and fro,
And with one heart the people pray ;
　　And this is home below.

And higher, in the House of God,
　　Seven lamps before the Throne,
The golden vials of odours sweet,
　　The voice of praise alone ;
With the belovèd, the redeemed,
　　Whose toil and tears are done,—
And this is in the Father's Home
　　That waits for everyone.

O Priest, whom men unkindly judged
　　Too fixed on rule and rite,
In this thine hour no ritual comes
　　To help thee through this night ;

None but the Everlasting Arms
   Support thee with their might,
None but the unseen Comforter
   Upholds thy soul in flight.

For thee no priest, nor passing bell,
   No holy oil or wine,
No prayer to speed the parting soul,
   No sacred word or sign ;
Long as thou hast by dying beds
   Ministered things divine,
Nor voice nor hand of earthly friend
   May minister to thine.

There is none other left but Thou,
   O Jesus, now give ear !
Far off is every help and hope,
   O Jesus, now draw near !
The heart is sinking and the flesh,
   O Jesus, save and hear !
Darkness and death—Oh, show Thy Face,
   O Jesus, Lord, most dear !

One kneeleth in his chamber,
　　Near midnight, at his prayer,
He feels a cold breath suddenly,
　　A presence in the air :
The white wraith flits before his eyes,
　　Awe-stricken and aware ;—
Yet till the morrow all unknown
　　Whose visiting was there.

No funeral tapers round thee burn,
　　No hand thy bed to dress,
No watchers kneeling round in prayer
　　And tears of tenderness.
The vigil and the fast are kept
　　Beside thee none the less,
By the dumb creatures in their love
　　And living faithfulness.

The deerhound and the terrier
　　Lie watching foot and head,
They only left of all on earth
　　To guard thy dying bed.

Two nights and days the searchers toil,
  The trackless wastes they tread,
In howling darkness, storm, and snow,
  Until they find the dead.

Thy feet are bruised upon the rocks,
  In struggle stiff and sore,
Thy corpse is frozen in the snow,
  With snow-wreaths mantled o'er ;
Thy face is calm,—the smile of one
  Remembering pain no more ;—
Their hearts were lightened of a load,
  Seeing the look it wore.

Ill-omened Pass ! laid under ban
  By curse from sire to son,—
The elemental powers have raved
  O'er torrent and o'er stone ;
Untamed and hostile hitherto,
  At last their worst is done,
A holier death has hallowed thee, —
  The Cross its place has won.

F

The funeral barge is on its way
    Across the pearly seas ;
One great white sea-bird flies before,
    With waving wings of peace ;
All shrouded white, the mountain-heights
    Still silently increase ;
Thy violet pall with flakes that fall
    Has grown snow-white as these.

They wait within the city,
    Stricken with grief, to lay
Their dead within St. Alban's,
    For one sad night and day.
Around thy bier the music wails,
    Thy people weep and pray ;
Thy mourners fill the streets on foot,
    Along the funeral way.

    .   .   .   .

O soul, that hast already passed
    Beyond this earthly bourn,
In London, in the narrow streets
    They miss thee, and they mourn ;

Thy face still haunts the holy house
   Where thou wilt not return ;
The hearts are aching day by day,
   With whom thou didst sojourn.

Is not thy sleep the smoother
   Because of hearts that ache?
Is not thy rest the deeper,
   That thy own heart did break?
Because to-day the sick and sad
   Are weeping for thy sake,
Surely their sighs have gone before,
   Thy bed in heaven to make.

To fast among the hungering,
   To serve among the poor,
To toil among the weary,
   Among the sick endure ;
To intercede for sinners,
   The tempted to secure :—
Thy lifelong path of pilgrimage,
   Most strait, most steep, most sure.

Sleep on in Christ.   'O Lamb of God!'
   Resounds the Passion hymn ;
And heaven is opened, and we join
   The song of Seraphim :
One Presence fills, unites, transforms,
   Beneath these arches dim,
And they who wake, and they who sleep,
   Together live in Him.

THE GLASTONBURY THORN.

My son, thou sayest that thy life
   Is past its blossom time,
And thou hast neither fruit nor flower
   To show for all its prime ;

That thou hast watched and waited long,
   Nor spared to toil and pray,
And nought for all thy strife remains,
   But to be cast away.

Now listen what to me befell
   When all the year was past,
And in the winter what a grace
   Was brought to me at last.

For I was old, and all my house
 Were sleeping in the tomb,
When came the Word of God to me
 To leave my fathers' home.

I took my staff, and all alone
 I wandered to the west ;
A long and weary pilgrimage,
 Till God should bid me rest.

I passed by sea, I passed by land,
 I found strange folk and wild,
Until one day before my feet
 This Vale at sunset smiled.

The voice within spake suddenly,
 ' Here is thy place to dwell : '
I struck my staff into the ground,
 And here I built my cell.

I cleared a little space of earth
   Beside it either hand,
And planted in my garden plot
   The flowers of Holy Land.

Oh, sweet and soft with mist and rain
   Is all this island air ;
The little birds among the boughs
   Make music everywhere.

And when the streams in Spring unbind,
   Trickling the moors across,
The violets blue, the violets white,
   Are hidden in the moss.

The people came about my door,
   A simple woodland race,
And many a meal I shared with them
   In many a dwelling-place.

I spake to them of Christ the Lord,
   And of the things I knew ;
They listened, and they made no sign,
   No faith among them grew.

But soon my garden flowers took root
   With little care or toil,
And flourished through the summer months
   Upon the stranger soil.

Anemones in April days
   Of silver shower and shine
Were messengers from scarlet fields
   Of spring in Palestine.

And starry-pointed, white and gold,
   The pale narcissus head,
Along the shady bank in May,
   A foreign fragrance shed.

The rosemary put forth in June
   Her shoots both sweet and strong ;
I thought of burning rocky paths
   The desert sides along.

Oh, glorious white as heaven's own light,
   The Lily rose, a Queen :
A sun by day, a star by night,
   Glimmering my prayers between.

And when the hot and cloudless sky
   Lay over field and fold,
In August, in the harvest time,
   Flamed forth the marigold.

O Mary! Mary! at thy name
   My head in dreams is bowed ;
I muse upon thy face with thoughts
   I cannot speak aloud,

The far-off years roll back, my soul
  Across the bitter sea
Returns, and there is only one
  Day of all days for me.

O Mary ! Mary ! for my loss
  I mourn until I die ;
The very thieves and murderers had
  A better place than I.

Yet I too had my turn at last,
  I who awoke too late ;
The lowest of thy servants still
  Outside the door may wait,

And find forgiveness in his task ;
  Yea, even unto me
Was granted gift my heart must keep
  In mute humility.

O Mary ! Mary ! I have seen !
    It cannot pass away ;
Thy face is living in my heart
    For ever, night and day.

Oh, on one night of wondrous light,
    Thy Babe upon thy knee,
When first He smiled, O mother mild,
    One Joseph stood by thee.

But I, another Joseph, stood
    Beside thee at the end ;
And when thine arms took back their own,
    Did I thy will attend.

Another night—oh, such a night
    Again earth will not see !—
For that night's sake forget me not,
    Until I come to thee !

I wander far, I lose myself ;—
　　What was the flower, the last,
That told me that the summer days
　　In this green land were past?

I think it was the myrtle soft,
　　I sheltered by the wall,
That flower of fate that blooms so late,
　　For maiden's coronal.

But when the time of flowers was past,
　　And Autumn leaves were sere,
Darkness drew on, and all the wold
　　With wailing winds was drear.

Early the Winter settled down,
　　The snow fell thick and deep,
The birds were hushed, the frozen rills
　　Were bound in glassy sleep.

And when at last drew nigh at hand
   The holy Christmas Eve,
A pathless wilderness of white
   Was all I could perceive.

I was alone, and not a step
   For many weeks had crossed
The buried moors, and I of men
   Forgotten seemed, and lost.

My food was spent ; for many days
   I had not broken fast ;
A little bird whose breast was red
   Had shared my crumbs—the last.

And now it seemed my time was come
   My labour to forsake ;
And sadly and in tears I knelt,
   And to my Master spake,—

'Lord, Thou hast set me here to sow
  The seed of faith for Thee ;
I sow in vain, I may not reap,
  Nor blade, nor corn I see.

'Thou callest me, and I must come
  Out of Thy garden ground,
With empty hands, and incomplete,
  Once more defaulting found.

'I know I shall forget my fault,
  When once I see Thy face ;
But, Lord, this is one bitter hour
  For the lost time of grace.'

Then at midnight, all silently,
  A spirit drew me forth ;
The three bright stars high overhead
  Were pointing to the North.

But a strange glow was in the air,
Vibrating sparks and strings,
And all the midnight was alive
With throbbing souls of things.

A quivering pulse of blood-red flame
Leapt up the heavenly height,
And soft and swift the rosy fire
Played in and out the night.

And all the world was lighted up,
I could not see from whence ;
I heard strange music in my ears,
I could not catch its sense.

The snow blushed crimson fitfully,
Like water turned to wine ;
I stepped into the open air,
And saw a wondrous sign.

For there my staff of pilgrimage,
   That in the ground stood fast,
Had shot into a living stem,
   Whose boughs were outward cast ;

And every branch was quick with leaf,
   And bud and flower and thorn ;
Beneath my gaze in still amaze
   The opening blooms were born.

O tree so bright 'mid snowy white,
   How didst thou smile on me :
The Master at the Feast to-night
   Hath not forgotten thee !

And when the Northern Lights had died,
   And night lay still and deep,
My eyes for very blissfulness
   Did close themselves in sleep.

I cannot tell what voices near
   In sleep conversed with mine ;
I do not know if angels came
   To bring me bread and wine.

But I lived on, I wanted not,
   I was not left alone ;
Our Master needs no other help
   When He would feed His own.

And the next spring, at Easter-tide,
   When the soft ferns unrolled,
And all the moorland sea of gorse
   Tossed its fresh waves of gold,

A thousand souls with one accord
   Came to the water's side,
And bowed themselves beneath the Sign
   Of Christ the Crucified.

G

And since that day a thousandfold
   The word has borne increase;
This fair and fruitful country lies
   All in one bond of peace.

They have not seen what I have seen,
   They have not touched the Hand ;
Blessèd are they, because by faith
   They love and understand.

O Lord, Thy purpose does not fail,
   The work is Thine alone ;
All times are harvest times with Thee :
   Enough, to be Thine own.

LONDON STREETS

G 2

'*TO A GREAT AND GOOD PHYSICIAN.*'

GOD hears to-day, and every day, for thee
Blessings and prayers uncounted ; therefore hear
Once for thyself, to greet thee this New Year,
    What He hears always :—little though it be
That words can tell.   We thank Him for thy life,
Fulfilled in one strong, simple, selfless strife
With pain and ill ; that, never taking breath
For one hour's ease, wrestles all day with death,
And conquers in His Name ; and for the power
For soul and body's aid, that is thy dower,—
The mighty gift of healing, half of God,
And half of some steep journey nobly trod,
Some sublime hour of sacrifice in youth,
Where the two ways met,—this world's praise, and
    Truth.

Is not the time of trial without fear
Because the comfort of thy voice is near?
Have we not known how, all these years gone
    by,
Wherever called thee the most hopeless cry,
Wherever want most sad, and pain most sore,
    Wherever most thy heart was pierced and rent,
Through the dark hours thy steadfast watchings
    wore,
    The touches of thy tenderness were spent,
Till from the saved, the succoured, the consoled,
One blessing wraps thy name a thousandfold ?

    Ah, to how many a man, like Hercules,
Hast thou brought home out of the gates of
    death
    The best-belovèd, and joined hands of these
That parted hopeless ; — or brought back the
    breath
Which even to the last had ebbed away
In little, lovely, moaning forms that lay
Chill on their mothers' bosoms ! Who shall say

Of what deliverances from what despairs
How many still are mindful in their prayers,
And still remember thee by!   At thy door
Even now what anxious faces evermore
Wait for the pity of thine eyes to cross
The story of their sickness or their loss ;
And no one goes away without some balm,
The pain made softer, or the fear more calm.
What restless forms to-day are lying, bound
On sick-beds, waiting till the hour come round
That brings thy foot upon the chamber stair,
Impatient, fevered, faint, till thou art there,
The one short smile of sunshine to make light
The long endurance of another night.

But of thy loving-kindness and thy care,
Hope, that thy footsteps follows everywhere,
Skill without measure, patience without fail,
Each   one   who   knows   thee   knows   a   separate
    tale ;
But only God knows all.—And if to some
(Are they indeed His best-beloved ?) there come

Hours of severer proof, and furnace-tried,

Which may not be cut short nor turned aside,—

When the art fails then the love triumphs more ;—

The last and best of gifts is yet in store.

Through uttermost extremity of pain,

Through darkness of deep waters, comes a strain

(The words return, the sense is mazed and dim),

'And there appeared an Angel, strengthening
    him.'

And thy face is the vision, and thy voice

    Is soft above the tempest, though it close

    Over one sinking in slow fires.   Who knows

How many hearts for evermore rejoice

For that revealing what a friend may be,

For that upholding they have had of thee

In that unspoken, solemn fellowship !

This blessing go with thee from heart and
    lip :—

Because for our sake, us the sufferers,

    Thou makest of thy moments and thy hours

From sunrise unto sunset ministers

    Unspared, unwearied, unto needs of ours,—

(From sunset unto sunrise who shall say
How often?) still foregoing day by day
The common ease and pleasure of the way,
Without self-pity and without regret
Wholly to thy heroic labour set,—
May God repay thee better than thy loss,
And such stray streaks as cannot choose but
    cross
The daily toil and tedium of thy track
Yield unto thee a sevenfold sunshine back !

    The grace of God upon thee, may'st thou feel
The shortened slumber and the hasty meal
Refresh thee as a Sacrament ;—thy sense
Be quickened into rapture more intense
Because thy joys are fewer ;—and the green
Valleys be fairer because far between.
The first white flashing of a swallow's wing,
Glimpses of pear-trees between walls in spring,
The morning air from new-mown fields in June,
The water-lilies on a Sabbath noon,

The solemn river-sunsets through the smoke,
The first reviving smile from eyes awoke
Out of Death's shadow unto life again,—
Be sweeter unto thee than other men.

    And because mortal sorrow needs must fall
On all men, and the highest most of all,
And some sharp struggle crowns each perfecting,
And that our lower love no shield can bring
    Between thee and the higher Love to stand,
That strikes for Love's own sake unfaltering,—
    Therefore when thou too stretchest out thy hand
For help, when thy need cometh, doubt, or pain,
Or loss, or other anguish of this earth,
And though we died for thee our death were vain,
And though we gave all it were nothing worth,
And of the many thousands whom thy face
Hath comforted, can none return the grace,
Being less than thee,— may the one Higher One
Do to thee even as thou to us hast done,
O Soother of our sorrows !   May'st thou see,
Steadfastly gazing towards Eternity,

The heavens opened, and at God's right hand
With the same smile as once thy Master stand ;—
Nor only so, but come down from His place,
And stand beside thee, and His arms embrace
Nor ever let thy hand go, holding fast,
Till all the tyranny be overpast.

New Year's Day.

WORKING-GIRLS IN LONDON.

'Is NOT this the time of flowers,
    And of birds that sing?'
'Here we know the days and hours,
    Not the Spring.'

'Is not this the age for pleasure,
    And for holidays?'
'We have neither ease nor leisure,
    Work always.'

'Are not ripe fruits now in season,
    Honey, cream, and cake?'
'Daily bread for us is reason
    Thanks to make.'

' Are not these the days for playing
    On the garden-grass ? '
' We, our daily work delaying,
    Starve, alas ! '

' Are not these the nights for wearing
    Robes of gossamer ? '
' Summer finds us burdens bearing,
    Spite of her.'

' Are not cool streams flowing whitely,
    Water-lily lit ? '
' Here within close walls we nightly
    Stifling sit.'

' Is not this the month for lying
    In the green leaves' shade ? '
' Summer breezes fresh are flying,
    Fast we fade.'

'Will not Love come here to-morrow,
    For bridegroom and bride?'
'Here Love meaneth pain and sorrow
    Multiplied.'

'Is not this the time of roses,
    Opening red and bright?'
'In the Chapel one reposes,
    Shut and white.'

'If of good things life bereft us,
    What avails the rest?'
'Still the better things are left us,
    And the best.'

'Are not some among you living
    Who can cheer the way?'
'Yes, their lives in service giving,
    Day by day.'

' Would you not with your rich neighbour
  Change, and cast off care ? '
' Christ our poverty and labour
  Chose to share.'

' Refuge have you none, unholpen,
  From the strife and din ? '
' Yes, the Church stands always open,
  Hushed within.'

' Is there not one hour suspended
  From the hard world's wrong ? '
' Softly sounds when day is ended
  Evensong.'

' Would you for fine houses rather
  Leave your chambers bare ? '
' Still in secret speaks Our Father
  To us there.'

'Are the days not long and dreary,
　　And the years afar?'
'Leaning on Thy breast Thy weary
　　Children are.'

'In your conflict have you never
　　Recompense for loss?'
'Yes, One Presence with us ever
　　Bears our cross.'

'O young feet, ye can but falter
　　On your road at length!'
'Still we kneel before the Altar
　　For fresh strength.'

'Have not some, O faithful daughters,
　　Sunk beneath the wave?'
'One we know in the deep waters,
　　Swift to save.'

' Are there not dark hours, too lonely
    For all help, at last ? '
' Through the darkest ones Christ only
    Holds us fast.'

DIVES.

O LAZARUS, between us lies
  A gulf which neither yet can pass ;
And yet one speaks, and one replies,
  Between us close no walls of brass ;
My life is lost, my soul undone ;
But Abraham calls me still his Son.

Thy brother too ! Year after year,
  In this deep dungeon of the dead,
Have we not soul to soul grown near,
  By interwoven fateful thread,
Remembering how our days have run
Together, underneath the sun ?

Thine eyes upon me used to wait
　With a mute pleasure and caress ;
As I went in and out my gate
　They almost smiled for gentleness.;
They seemed to thank me passing by,
For sight of one so fine as I.

Those patient eyes reproached me not,
　Their envy poisoned not my good,
They seemed to say, ' So mean my lot,
　I cannot serve thee as I would.'
I took the will, and was content
With thy admiring wonderment.

Thou hadst no sister, Lazarus,
　Thou hadst no friend of human kind ;
Thy desolate heart was turned to us,
　Some solace for its love to find ;
The tender flattery I could read,
But nothing of the piteous need.

I and my brethren were to thee
   Thy pageant, freely thine to share ;
Thou in thy mouldering rags might'st see
   How cool fine linen was to wear ;
And every day a sumptuous feast
I spread before thine eyes at least.

Thou didst my every sense offend,
   And yet I sometimes looked thy way,
I knew thee for a humble friend,
   I gave thee leave to see me gay ;
Gracious and generous to excuse
Thy want of worth, thy want of use.

Out of my luxury's excess
   I spared no single drop for thee ;
Out of thy utter nakedness
   Thou gavest heavenly gift to me ;
For ever seeming to implore
My pardon that it was not more.

' Most worshipful, I cannot serve,
    I am a blot in thy fair sight,
No slave's least portion I deserve,
    I taint the air, I mar the light : '
Yet I forgave thee all this wrong,
And sometimes threw a dole along.

O Lazarus, how fiercely ached
    Thy burning sores the whole day long !
How was thy bitter thirst unslaked !
    No drop of water cooled thy tongue.
And yet my hard heart did not melt ;—
I know it now, for I have felt.

How meek and hopeless thy desire
    For crumbs that from my table fell ;
O Lazarus, the flakes of fire
    Fall on my heart, in rain of hell !
Oh, the slow pangs, day after day
Thou starving at my side away !

And yet I missed thee from thy place,
  My daily life was incomplete,
My pompous march had lost its grace,
  The meal unwatched became less sweet ;
By thy humility my pride
No longer could be satisfied.

We are not fixed so far apart
  But that I knew thy face again,
Thy patient face that held my heart
  By one last link not snapt in twain :
It seemed a simple thing at first
To call for thee to slake my thirst.

Should I not send thee to and fro,
  My messenger with willing feet,
Back to my father's house to go,
  Along the well-remembered street ?
Wouldst thou not hasten, glad and proud,
So much promoted and allowed ?

And thou, I know—yes, thou art not
   Less loving than in days of old ;
Thy wistful watch was not forgot ;
   I seem to hear the sigh that told
Thou too wast frustrate of thy task :—
To minister thou still dost ask.

Was this indeed the face I saw
   So carelessly, so many days ?
Oh, blessèd be the fires that draw
   The veil from my besotted gaze !
Thou angel, that I now see plain,
Whom I did never entertain !

Too late for me, too late it is !
   Dogs were more pitiful than I ;
I never gave thee any kiss,
   Thy unanointed wounds were dry :
But oh, in vain, how many years
Have I not washed them with my tears !

But, O my Lazarus, it is gone ;
   For ever past is all thy pain ;
If for one hour I might atone,
   I would not bring it back again :
My everlasting loss I bear,
Once mine, but once, for love and care !

Lazarus, my Lazarus, from afar
   Still toward me turned thy face I see,
Me from thy smile doth none debar,
   Thine eyes look out to comfort me ;
Thy hand a sterner law controls :
It is not set between our souls.

How can I ask thee to forgive,
   Who of my crimes no reckoning took ?
Who by a monster used to live,
   And yet couldst bear on him to look ?
Whose spirit dwelt its griefs above,
And only felt the angels' love ?

We cannot now be reconciled,
　　Where strife has never entered in ;
Thy charity, thy suffering mild,
　　Working with God thy peace to win,
Have worked this miracle as well,—
To save a soul alive in hell.

And still behind thee seems to grow
　　Another, dimly like to thee,
Whose looks meet mine, till scarce I know
　　If it were thou or it were He
Who all those years lay on thy bed,
Unloved, unknown, uncomforted.

Weep not for me, O Lazarus !
　　On Abraham's bosom thou dost hide
Thy tears that flow to see me thus :
　　Must we not patient both abide ?
My sins are greater than my doom :
That which I was, may hell consume !

Through all the torment stern and strange,
   I feel, as winter feels the spring,
In me and all around a change,
   Some far-off day the years will bring :
Perchance thy prayers have brought it near ;
God's will be done, both there and here !

And then, O Lazarus, thou shalt come,
   And to thy Master draw me near ;
It *is* thy hand shall lead me home,
   It is thy voice shall give me cheer ;
And thou too shalt have thy desire
Fulfilled at last, although by fire.

By all our past that we have earned,
   May it not be that thou and I,
Together yet, both hearts that yearned,
   Thou, O belovèd, set on high,
And I within the lowest place,
May serve one Master face to face?

Lazarus, my Lazarus, we will go
   Together, I on thee will wait ;
That souls made wiser by our woe
   May learn their lesson not too late.
What need of words between us now ?
We know each other, I and thou.

FAREWELL HYMN FOR BISHOP SMYTHIES OF EAST AFRICA.

St. Alban's, October 10th, 1888.

Christ has called thee.   On thy mission
   Thou art going forth to-day ;
Home and country, ease and safety,
   These are bonds to hold and stay :
Stronger is the hand constraining ;—
   Christ is calling,—come away !

Down the jungle-swamps of fever,
   Down the dark slave-driver's track,
Through the roaring of the lions,
   Through the Unknown, shapeless, black,
Through the savage hosts of slaughter,
   Christ is leading ;—look not back !

Dearer than all else, He draws thee
  Where no stream of gladness runs ;
He has given thee His message
  To His most forsaken sons ;
Filled thy heart with His own pity
  For His sheep, the long-lost ones.

Some have gone before, and fallen,
  Not until their work could stand :—
Follow, to fill up their places,
  With the torch from hand to hand,
Till the African vast blackness
  Glitters with a beacon-band !

Lights are shining in dark places,
  Seeds are springing from the tomb,
O'er the desert-wastes already
  Breaks the Rose of Martyrdom ;
Saints we knew with dusky faces
  Smile upon us out of home.

Speed thee !   Here are tears of parting,
   Friend looks sadly upon friend ;
Shall we here once more have meeting ?
   What shall be His crown to send ?
In the peace He gives thou goest ;
   God be with thee to the end !

THE SHADE OF CHATTERTON.

BROOKE STREET, HOLBORN.

THE church on winter afternoons
    Is warm, is dark,
The cold wind whistles down the street,
    Sighs and moans,—hark !
Out of a hundred years of waste,
    Of seas without a mark,
The dove on weary wing beats back
    To the ark.

Oh, I am poorer than you all,
    More weak, more thin ;
Oh, I go mourning all alone,
    Unsaved from sin.

I will go out before your Feasts
And glorious Songs begin ;
Let me in when the lights are low,
Let me in !

Oh, the cold fogs, for those who rest
Not in the tomb !
Oh, it is cold along the street,
In sleet and gloom !
Oh, it was cold a hundred years
Up in the haunted room !
I sat and shivered comfortless
For my doom.

I left a name, a short sad tale,
A mournful shade ;
Some words of pity followed me,
Men praised, none prayed ;
Careless, a withered laurel leaf
Upon my grave they laid ;
Then they forgot me, till you came
To my aid.

You built a church for sanctuary,
       '   Thither I fled ;
You worshipped there, I listened to
       The words you said ;
You kept the vigils of the year,
       Remembering the dead ;
You wrote my name, by all who pass
       To be read.

A Cross upon the door drives ill
       Spirits away ;
I clasped it close, it was the first
       That came my way ;
I kissed it weeping,—' Oh, how long
       I waited for this day ! '
I came unbidden with the rest,
       Let me stay !

I haunt the empty space between
       The font and door ;
When you go home I stay on guard,
       Your janitor ;

I

I do not sleep at nights, but they
    Seem shorter than before ;
A shadow in the shadow I lie
    On the floor.

Far off I see your Altar Lights,
    I hear your Song ;
The church is filled, but I am left
    Out of the throng.
Oh, I am Thine, though spurned of Thee !
    Have I then done Thee wrong ?
Out of the deeps I call on Thee,—
    For how long ?

I suffer in your midst, so much
    At least I share ;
I love, though I am not beloved,
    My soul lies bare :
The pale ghosts cannot be forbid
    To pray, and wail in prayer ;
You could not sweep away my sighs
    From the air.

I do not know your Christmas Day,
    I keep your Lent ;
You know the Father's face and hand,
    Above you bent ;
If He would have me for His slave,
    I would be well content ;
With bleeding heart I kneel with you,
    Penitent.

All glorious things within me stirred,
    As in the bud ;
Heroic deeds and wonderful
    Throbbed in my blood ;
Dim and wild echoes came to me
    Along time's rolling flood ;
I wove them into words, I half
    Understood.

The creed of Christ was spoken round,
    I knew it not.
Wild music sounded in my brain,
    My heart was hot ;

The fires of hell, the fires of heaven
    Were mingled in this spot ;
I had no sign, it seemed as if
    Heaven forgot.

O sorrow of fate ! the seasons keep
    Their time on earth :
Why should the seasons of the heavens
    Fail of their mirth ?
Of daisies and of primroses
    The May-Day hath no dearth ;
But the Flower of the Gods in January
    Came to birth.

Faces that were unseen by me,
    Voices unheard !
I would have waited on your will,
    For one kind word.
I could have lived ! I would have been
    Your happy singing-bird ;
You should have been more glad for me,
    More heart-stirred.

I pass you, though you see me not,
    Along the street ;
I watch your coming as for friends,
    Kind eyes I meet :
The pavement echoes with the tread
    Of ministering feet ;
In the grey morning I am first
    Out to greet.

O boys to-day ! in Bands of Hope,
    In Guild, in Roll,
One of your days of everyday
    Had saved my soul ;
One word of all the words you hear
    Had made my spirit whole ;
I would have begged your wasted crumbs
    For my dole.

You hunger, but you will not starve
    Without a friend ;
There are dark times,—you have a hope
    Lights up the end ;

You toil, but others toil with you,
For you their lives they spend ;
You fall,—hands are stretched out to you,
To amend.

O kindly led, be kind to me,
Comfort me too !
I was as young as you, give me
A place with you.
Of all the gifts so freely given,
Leave me at least a few ;
Spare me sometimes out of your prayers
One or two.

O priests, who daily minister,
Give me some sign !
For me who have but tears to drink,
Where you pour wine.
Is there no bond of fellowship,
Our hearts to intertwine ?
When you confess the people's sins,
Speak for mine !

I am no longer desolate,
    I have a home ;
Familiar footsteps come and go
    Amidst the gloom :
Yours is the Children's Bread,— to wait
    The Master exiles some :
I shall be watching here, when next
    He shall come.

MISCELLANEOUS.

THE CROCUS.

Out of the frozen earth below,
Out of the melting of the snow,
  No flower, but a film, I push to light ;
No stem, no bud,—yet I have burst
The bars of winter, I am the first,
  O Sun, to greet thee out of the night !

Bare are the branches, cold is the air,
Yet it is fire at the heart I bear,
  I come, a flame that is fed by none :
The summer hath blossoms for her delight,
Thick and dewy and waxen-white,
  Thou seest me golden, O golden Sun !

Deep in the warm sleep underground
Life is still, and the peace profound :
    Yet a beam that pierced, and a thrill that smote
Called me and drew me from far away ;—
I rose, I came, to the open day
    I have won, unsheltered, alone, remote.

No bee strays out to greet me at morn,
I shall die ere the butterfly is born,
    I shall hear no note of the nightingale ;
The swallow will come with the break of green,
He will never know that I have been
    Before him here when the world was pale.

They will follow, the rose with thorny stem,
The hyacinth stalk,—soft airs for them ;
    They shall have strength, I have but love :
They shall not be tender as I,—
Yet I fought here first, to bloom, to die, ˙
    To shine in his face who shines above.

O glory of Heaven, O Ruler of Morn,

O Dream that shaped me, and I was born

 In thy likeness, starry, and flower of flame ;—

I lie on the earth and to thee look up,

Into thy image will grow my cup,

 Till a sunbeam dissolve it into the same.

THE SIEGE OF STRASBURG.

THE siege of Strasburg !—for in those dread days,
Strasburg the Virgin stood before her foes
More helpless, hopeless, than Andromeda ;
Chained to her pile, but with fair-fronting eyes,
And breast bare to the pitiless storm that smote,
And smote her bleeding but inviolate limbs ;
While round and over her the iron hail
By day fell, and the red rain fell by night,—
And knew no succour coming nor to come ;
And still endured, and made no sign, and said,
' The end is not yet come, and day by day
My agony shall stay their feet from France ;
Therefore I die by inches.'   And all knew
Her doom was on her ; and the world without
Sent never a message to her, nor farewell,

Nor any eye met hers but the ringed eyes
Of the grey cannon, round against her set,
That marked each shuddering and each streak of fire,
As the bombs struck her and she still endured.

But once for mercy spake aloud, as when
She sent her girls and children to the gates,
Having kissed them as who should not meet again,
And said, heart-broken, 'Let but these depart.'
And back the answer came to her, 'Too late !
Die all—or yield—together '   So they stayed.
And as the fire waxed fiercer round her heart,
Prayed yet once more in her extremity,
'Send us some draught of sleep, some fever balm,
For those who lie with lips and limbs on fire
Within our hospitals !'   And yet once more
The answer was sent back to her, 'Too late !
No more till the surrender !'   Then she ceased,
And prayed no more to man, nor yet to God ;
And all her thousands set themselves to death
Within her walls, and starved to skeletons,
Or sickened in the darkness underground,

And came forth but for burial of their dead.
And ever overhead the heaven was brass,
And through the empty streets the sheets of fire
From house to house by daylight scorched and leapt,
While the continuous rocking roar was yet
O'ercrashed a moment as the roofs fell in.
And week by week the faces that remained
Grew greyer, ghastlier ; and her soldiery
Dropped at their posts, and mangled limbs were strewn
On their own hearths, and, as the shells came through,
Her little children in their mothers' arms
Were torn to pieces, and her babes were born
Between the boomings as their fathers died.

THE FIRST OF JUNE.

LAST night I lay upon my bed,
   With sinking heart alone ;
Long weeks, long months I so have lain,
   Weeping and making moan.

All May has passed ; I hardly know
   If swift spring-rains have stirred,
There hath not broken through the dark
   One flash of flower or bird.

But sleep stole on me unawares,
   Even on me at last ;
Though drop by drop the minutes faint
   Like hours at midnight passed.

K

Short was the sleep, since even now
  The summer dawn is nigh ;
But health and healing it has brought ;
  I wake—but is it I ?

I feel no more these limbs of pain,
  I draw no sobbing breath,
Life has come back to me at last,
  And God remembereth.

How many years since I have known
  A waking glad like this :
Nay, can I once recall an hour
  So peaceful as it is ?

I have forgotten when it was
  That I such ease have known ;
What hinders me from rising up
  And going forth alone ?

Why should I too not wander out
   Through the sweet morning mist,
And see the sunrise out of doors,
   That all my life I missed ?

The house is hushed and sleeping,
   My footsteps noiseless fall,
From door to door, from stair to stair :
   Peace rest within on all !

The door is opened easily,
   I stand beneath the sky ;
The old watch-dog remembers me,
   Nor stirs as I go by.

Here on the lawn my children play ;
   Across the stile I pass,
Out of the dewy garden
   Into the meadow grass.

The grass is cool and damp and tall,
　　It rustles to my knees :
Year after year does morning bring
　　Airs upon earth like these ?

As to the crimson East I turn
　　The rising sun to meet,
The clover and the daisies dim
　　All close about my feet.

The cuckoo gives the signal call
　　From hill to hill unseen,
From every side the hymn of birds
　　Fills all the fields between.

Down to the brook, across the bridge ;
　　Where deep and high and dank
The orchis heads crowd through the grass,
　　And leaning from the bank

The guelder-rose dips in the stream,
   And golden flags are hung,
Out of whose midst the water-hen
   Awakens with her young.

I have heard said, the kingfisher
   Was used to haunt this brook,
But seen no more of latter years :
   He comes again, for—look !—

The flashing of his wings goes by
   Almost against my face :
He is not shy to-day, within
   This willow-fringèd place.

The sun is up, the mist is cleared,
   All the still land lies fair ;
As up the sloping leas I pass,
   The sweetest grass grows there.

All in among the crowded lambs,
   They do not run away ;
The field-mice flit along the path,
   Like little friends at play.

The larks sing high in the blue sky
   As if in heaven they were ;
I too am free and full of glee
   Out in the open air.

And now I pass th' horizon hill
   That bounds my window-view ;
O house of love, O house of pain,
   For how long time ?—adieu.

Oh, I have wandered many a mile
   Through a country wild and sweet ;
I am not tired, I do not want
   To stay, or sit, or eat.

It seems as if at last the soul
    And body were reconciled ;
I think there once was such a day
    When I was a little child.

A wicket-gate leads to a wood,
    And as I enter through,
The speedwell from the bank looks up
    With eyes of heavenly blue.

The flowers smile up, the birds sing down,
    Come in, they sing and say ;
The wood is dark and fragrant-fresh
    With June's first hour and day.

I wander deep, I wander far
    Into the green wood's heart ;
I come unto an open space
    Where the low branches part.

Beyond the level summer lawn
　　The forest oak-trees spread ;
Under the stateliest of them all
　　The moss has made a bed.

Oh, on soft couches laid in vain
　　With aching limbs across,
How often have I dreamed of this —
　　A bed of earth and moss !

Here I will rest—Oh, everywhere
　　Is rest and health at last ;
How can such utter weariness
　　So suddenly be past?

The wood-doves murmur over my head,
　　Soon ! soon ! soon ! for a sign :
But who is this beside me
　　Whose eyes look into mine?

'Oh, can it be you come back at last?
  And where is it I meet with you?
Are not the waste wide waters
  Of Death between us two?'

'Oh, all these years, by night and day,
  I have watched beside the gate;
I have looked down the road that you would
    come,
  I have waited early and late;
I have been weary in Paradise,
  Oh, it was long to wait!

'Do you not know that you have come
  Across the waves in sleep?
And this is your birthday morning
  Together we will keep.'

THE IMPENITENT THIEF.

SAVE thyself first ! if Thou indeed
    Be Christ, the King of Israel,
Now is Thy time, Thy time of need,
    To help Thyself and us as well.
I will not own Thee Master thus,
Who canst not save Thyself nor us.

I do not call Thee Christ ; for me
    No Christ is, nor hath ever been ;
Long underfoot we trampled Thee,
    Now Thou hast equal place between.
'Thou lifted up from earth shalt draw
All men '—but not this one outlaw.

I do not call Thee Lord; if Thou
   Didst make this world, it was ill-made :
It is too late to save me now,
   Long, long ago I wanted aid.
I am no servant, no, nor friend,
Who did not find Thee till this end.

Thou didst not save me when my birth
   Doomed me to shame and misery,
Thou didst not save me when the earth
   Her misbegotten scorned in me,
Thou didst not save when my first crime
Drove me and fixed me to the slime.

The tortured men for hidden gold
   That made my pastime and my prey,
The children into slavery sold,
   The butchered corpses by the way,
The ravished maidens in despair,
Thou didst not save, I did not spare.

Thou wilt not save in days to come,
   No, not Thine own, Thine innocent ;
The lips that called on Thee are dumb
   In death, when all their cries are spent :
Thy little ones without a friend
Wail day and night, and none defend.

Gaunt, hollow-eyed, the millions pass
   In blank and fathomless despair ;
Imploring hands to heaven, alas !
   They lifted, but Thou wast not there ;
The sick, the starved, the shamed, the slave,
Thou didst not show Thyself to save.

I know Thee long, I saw the crowd
   That strove to touch Thy garment's hem,
The tears that flowed, the heads that bowed,
   I mocked at Thee, I mocked at them ;
Thy face I saw, Thy voice I heard,
Yet nothing in me spoke or stirred.

How many, who will call Thee Lord,
   Turn on their side again to sleep ;
Thy blood, Thy tears for them were poured,
   No need for them to bleed or weep :
They are content that Thou hast died ;
But I with Thee was crucified.

They fix their eyes on Thee for gain
   Of Thy completed sacrifice,
They buy their pleasure by Thy pain,
   Set free, for Thou hast paid the price ;
I go not free, I pay the cost,
Yet they are saved and I am lost.

Some stand afar, and some allowed
   Near—but no closer may they win.
Once on Mount Sinai in the cloud
   Moses alone might enter in :
Here on Mount Golgotha we Three,
Alone within the Agony.

' On Thy right hand, on Thy left hand,
 Within Thy kingdom, Lord, to sit ; '
So prayed she who has come to stand
 Here, where she little dreamed of it.
I have not asked nor prized the grace,
But I have first the left-hand place.

' To them for whom it is prepared.'
 How long ago? Have I been led
By eyes that knew, by hands that cared,
 Down all dark ways, until this dread
Accomplishment, and set on high
In this unlooked-for company ?

If Thou art Lord, and Thou didst choose
 Those who should drink this cup with Thee,
The saint, the friend Thou didst refuse,
 To lay Thy fatal hand on me ;
Peter with Jesus would have died,
Yet I am here, and he denied.

O Mother of Sorrows, in thy place!
   The sword is piercing through thy heart ;
The years ran on, the years apace,
   The slow hours rend thy soul apart ;
But through my flesh the nails are driven,
Part in thy pains to me is given.

Kings cast their crowns before Thy feet,
   Praying Thee, use us for Thy sake !
Earth's fairest for Thy service sweet
   Their bed among the vilest make ;
Saints spurn their flesh to share Thy lot ;—
Yet all of these approach me not.

I suffer with Thee to the last,
   I drink the dregs of all with Thee,
The world's Redeemer holds me fast
   Beside Him on His cross to be ;
But the Redemption He will win
Will touch me not, nor take me in.

Didst Thou exalt me to this height
  Of awful fellowship with Thee,
To cast me back into the night
  Of sin, and sin's satiety?
To point a moral and adorn
Thy triumph's tale, have I been born?

'With the same baptism baptized'
  As Thou Thyself, the worlds between,
I the most vile and most despised,
  I whom no water has made clean,
What meaning in my fate is found,
For me unwilling brought and bound?

None weep for me; no rudest pang
  Is spared, and no last cruelty:
Here to the whole world's gaze I hang,
  Whole generations gaze at me:
They will not pity me; but Thou—
I feel Thy pity on me now.

' Forgive, they know not what they do,'
  Though open wounds are plain to see ;
Dost Thou perchance forgive me too,
  Who have but flung hard words at Thee ?
Words are but little gain or loss
To Him who hangs upon the cross.

The hours are dark, the hours are slow,
  Their shadows are the shadow of fire ;
Yet in their flame some foul stains go,
  Some scales drop from me and expire.
Yea, I receive my deeds' reward,
Yea, here and now, some sight restored.

'The last shall be the first ;—the first
  Last '—ah ! who knoweth what swift flame
Eats out the heart of things accurst,
  Burns from the soul the shroud of shame ?
Who knoweth what new blood may run
In the new veins with Thee made one ?

O Crowned with thorns ! dost Thou infuse
   Through Suffering, Love itself in me ?
Apart from Thee I cannot choose ;
   Can I unloose my soul from Thee?
Between us Thou hast forged a bond
That reaches through the worlds beyond.

Thou speakest low, Thou speakest yet,
   O heart of mine, and can it be !
Are these my eyes with tears are wet?
   O voice that no one hears but me !
But between Thee and me alone
Some words have passed, some words are known.

What hast Thou said ?—Ah this shall be
   Recorded not in any page—
To me the lost, whose memory
   Accurst shall pass from age to age ?
This secret I with me shall keep
There where the just and unjust sleep.

THE SEASONS.

SPRING.

A VOICE comes nearer as the fresh winds sweep,
  And pierces through the dreaming of the Earth,
Wherein as ever, waking or asleep,
  She labours still for each revolving birth.
She knows afar the voice, through fields of air,
Of her, before whose coming, blue and fair
  The heavens enlarge themselves, and softly meet
With the horizon hills of shadowy blue
Whence run the loosened waters, azure too,
  While the blue violets spring to kiss her feet.
Our hearts leap in us, as thou comest, Spring !
Joy runs before thee, thou whose touch can bring
All hidden life to its own conscious hour,
The breaking of its own form to the flower,

The swelling of its own heart to the bud,

And to the maiden's cheek the quicker blood.

   The waving wings of birds in unison

Before thee spread thy secret to the air,

And the winds sweep with it across the bare

   Boughs of the forest, till they too bear on

The rushing music of the wild south-west.

O first fair hours, shall not the last be best?

And here they come, the promise of the year,

Young dreams, young hopes, winged from another

     sphere.

Although their tender feet are on the flowers,

These budding wings must grow with growing hours ;

Yet stay with us awhile your fairy flight,

And make the whole way lovely with your light !

SUMMER.

SING me thy songs, O Summer ! let me hear,

   Now that the boughs are green, the winds are laid,

   Through the warm noonday silence of the shade,

The things thou hast to give, fulfilled and near.

A fire of poppies burns within the wheat,

And through my eyelids shoots its slumberous heat,

With dazzling images of all bright things;

The very dreams have folded their sweet wings,

As if they had arrived at their own shore,

And had no need to wander any more.

A scent of bean flowers comes across the breeze,

Filled with the busy murmur of the bees,

And all the distance lies in hazy gold;

And even as thou singest, I behold,

   Amid the leafy windings of the plain,

Some lane of roses leading lone and low

   Into a bower of bliss for me to gain,

Awaiting me until the sunset's glow.

The lilies and the hollyhocks stand tall

On the smooth lawn against the cottage wall,

The doves' white wings upon its low roofs brood,

And the great lime-trees guard its solitude.

Shall I not enter in, and be content,

Past the long rows of bees that homeward went?

They too have made their home about its door,

And hive for me their golden summer store.

AUTUMN.

WHERE is the promise of thy golden days,
  O Summer, of thy softly-fleeting hours?
Is this the end of thy delightful ways?
  The year is waning :—what is left for ours?
Through leafless branches chilly blows the air ;
Yet let us turn, our garnered wealth to share,
And comfort us with warmth of corn and wine,
Strengthening our hearts to meet the year's decline.
But where are thy heaped treasures manifold,
Thy purple fruitage, and thy sheaves of gold ?
The showers of spring, the sultry summer's sun
Have been before thee, and their part is done ;
What more is wanting to the harvest-home,
Pressed full and full, and plenty left to come?
Spring passed in hopes, and summer passed in dreams,
Thy passing should be glorious too, meseems.
What is this scanty fruit so poor, so cold,
Thy branches scatter, and thy fingers hold ?
Is this the measure but of one day's meal?
What for the sinking heart of days that steal

With lengthening shadows towards me, and the store

Of bounty that should overflow my door?

O purple hills, O purple wastes all bare,

Ye mock me, thinking of the days that were!

I stretch my empty hands in vain, in vain;—

    These idle hands that had in all the past

    Their own part waiting them :—and yet, at last,

Is it too late some working space to gain?

Are not these arms still strong?—Too well I know,

This is the time to reap, and not to sow.

WINTER.

O FLY for shelter, for the storm is near,

    The evil days are come, the wintry foe;

    Nothing avails us now, but such life-glow

As we have gleaned and gathered through the year.

O cruel Winter, with thy frowning face,

From thee there is no hope, no gift, no grace;

Already saved and sure our home must be,

Or now we perish, outcast, utterly.

But where, on all the desolate blasted plain,

Rises the refuge that our steps should gain?

Where is the guarded flame, the heaped hearthstone,

Which patient toil and thought have made our own,

Beneath the roof where winter winds howl past,

Yet cannot shake its doors and windows fast?

Alas, no work of hands, no warmth of heart

Have fenced for us the harbouring rest apart:

The frozen bed of earth, the snowy pall,

The last, the only birthright left of all.

Yet this world's utter loss is not the end:

Now, open, Heaven, and to our need descend!

O children of the air, fair hopes and dreams,

Whose light wings fluttered by the Spring's sweet
    streams,

'Twixt earth and heaven, have ye not heavenward
    grown,

Lifted by faith and prayer into your own

Ethereal likeness, and your wings at length

Grown into angels' pinions by the strength

Of trial, and of daily duty done,

Till now ye fly full-furnished every one,—

Come, dear companions of our vanished year,
And bear us to your own immortal sphere !

Alas ! alas ! and is it even ye,
Naked and shivering from the blast that flee
With earthbound limbs, and wings as tender still
As those that opened first at the first thrill
Of the Spring's touch,—our friend who brought us
    life ;—
  And now our enemy is here, with death ;
We have no weapons, no defence for strife,
  And all is over ;—this is our last breath :
Hopeless and homeless on the waste world driven,
And fallen back to Earth, tho' born for Heaven.

HAREBELLS.

THE bells are ringing and ringing,
   Little low bells on the earth ;
Sweet as a woodlark's wild singing,
   Little clear laughter and mirth.
The sunshine breaks, and all around
A streak of sky runs over the ground,
    Where the poor man's way is open still,
    The bells of England on heath and hill.

Lie and rest on the dry turf here,
A soft, soft flutter comes rustling near ;
    One eye-level of dazzling blue
    Dances and streams the wind's way through.
Slumber steals through the nodding band.

So, for an hour, dost thou dream, and say,

' I shall have my heart's desire to-day : '

Then rise and go, thou hast thy way ;

These are the bells of Fairy Land.

The statelier flowers may keep their pride,

We fear no footsteps, we do not hide ;

On the trodden turf of the waste roadside

   We are blown and beaten in breaths of blue ;

The wings of the gnat are not so thin ;

   But we smile in singing the wild days through,

We are here for any who care to win.

Close by is the city's smoke and din ;

   Even its children can walk so far,

   The poor, the sick, may reach where we are.

We too are lowly, we too are frail,

Therefore we too outlast and prevail.

Here, high up on the open hill,

The air of autumn is rude and chill :

The great star-thistle, the tormentil,

   Purple and gold on the bare hillside,

Cling to the earth with arms clasped wide,
As though they might never else abide ;
But the wind that sweeps the down on high
Scatters our light as it passes by,
Shakes out our peals of melody :
    These are the bells of Eventide.

The gold and the white open the year,
The iris and rose are no longer here,
The green of the woods is turning sere,
    The lily has bowed, it could not stand.
But the year's last flowers are tender and blue,
The flowers that are faithful when flowers are few,
We guard the path till the harvest is through :
    These are the bells of Holy Land.

Finest and frailest of all the flowers,
We are left alone in the autumn hours,
To bear the brunt of the storms and showers ;
    The skies above us are grey and sad :

But the hue of heaven to earth we bring,

But the heart of heaven in our bells we ring ;

Low, low, low,—are you listening ?

    The heart of heaven is gay and glad.

Come away, come away, come away !

The eyes of the angels are blue and grey.

    There is one coming down the crowded street,

He is passing out, he is coming this way,

Here, up here, where the winds are at play ;

    At the turn of the road you cannot but meet :

You will know his face, you will understand,

He need not speak, he will reach his hand,

Oh, the surprise, too sweet to say !

The bells are ringing in Angel Land.

One to go, and many to stay :

Each his turn,—you have come this way.

Why are we dancing here so gay ?

    Why has the music just begun ?

Like a peal of church-bells down they run,
Down, down, down, from a height away,
Thousands on thousands, one by one,
Each a spirit—off and away !
Do you not know, do you not see,
Blue as the breadths of the sky and sea,
The light of love, of eternity?
The bells are ringing in Heaven to·day !

PRINTED BY
SPOTTISWOODE AND CO., NEW-STREET SQUARE
LONDON

www.ingramcontent.com/pod-product-compliance
Lightning Source LLC
Chambersburg PA
CBHW020014030726
47500CB00002B/582